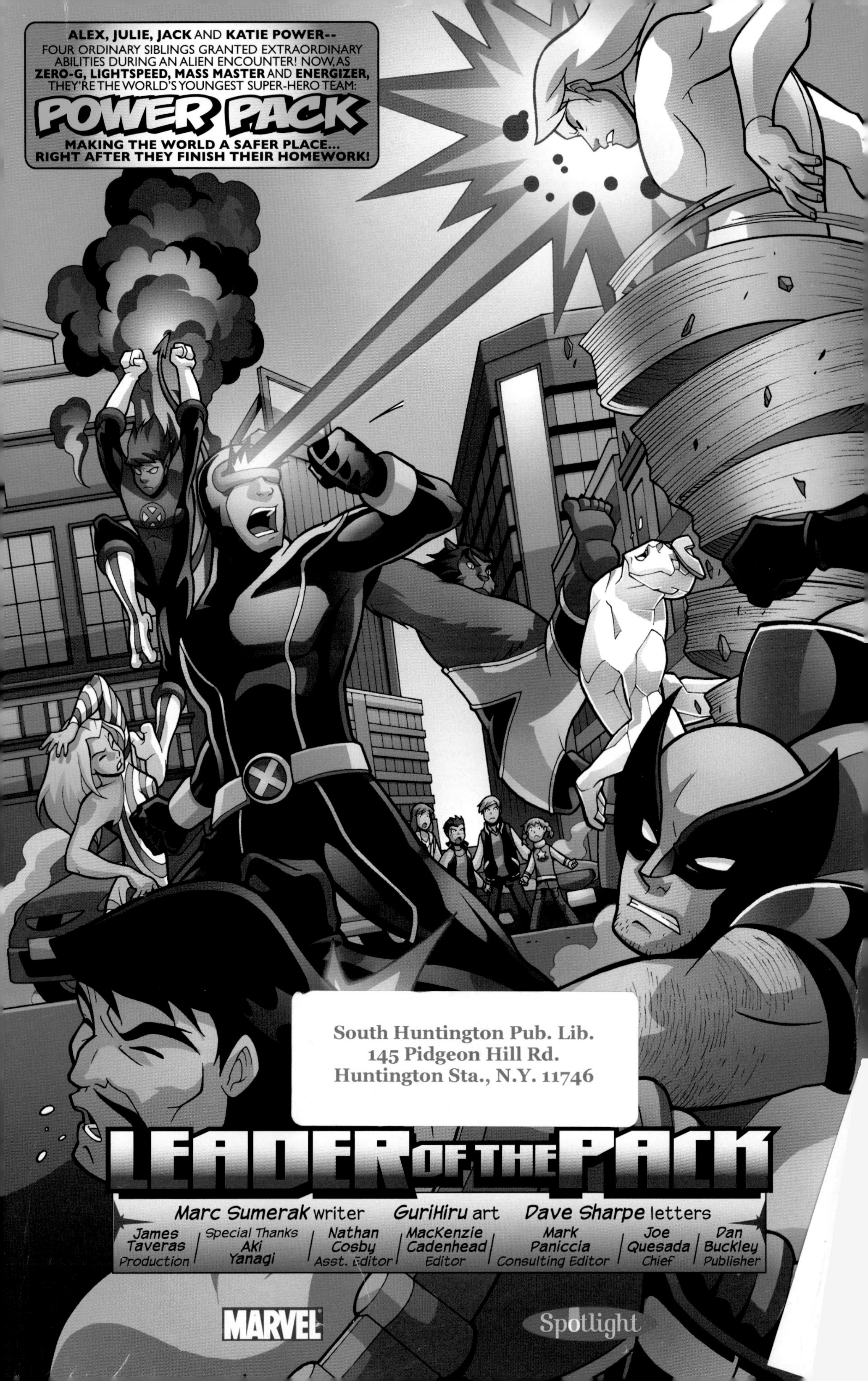
ALEX, JULIE, JACK AND KATIE POWER--
FOUR ORDINARY SIBLINGS GRANTED EXTRAORDINARY ABILITIES DURING AN ALIEN ENCOUNTER! NOW, AS ZERO-G, LIGHTSPEED, MASS MASTER AND ENERGIZER, THEY'RE THE WORLD'S YOUNGEST SUPER-HERO TEAM:
POWER PACK
MAKING THE WORLD A SAFER PLACE... RIGHT AFTER THEY FINISH THEIR HOMEWORK!
LEADER OF THE PACK
Marc Sumerak writer GuriHiru art Dave Sharpe letters
James Taveras Production | Special Thanks Aki Yanagi | Nathan Cosby Asst. Editor | MacKenzie Cadenhead Editor | Mark Paniccia Consulting Editor | Joe Quesada Chief | Dan Buckley Publisher
MARVEL
Spotlight

VISIT US AT
www.abdopublishing.com

Spotlight library bound edition © 2007. Spotlight is a division of ABDO Publishing Company, Edina, Minnesota.

MARVEL, and all related character names and the distinctive likenesses thereof are trademarks of Marvel Characters, Inc., and is/are used with permission. Copyright © 2006 Marvel Characters, Inc. All rights reserved. www.marvel.com

MARVEL, X-Men Power Pack: TM & © 2006 Marvel Characters, Inc. All rights reserved. www.marvel.com. This book is produced under license from Marvel Characters, Inc.

Cataloging Data

Sumerak, Marc
    Sumerak, Marc
    Leader of the pack / Marc Sumerak, writer ; GuriHiru, art ; Dave Sharpe, letters. -- Library bound ed.
       p. cm. -- (X-Men power pack)
    Summary: Marvel's youngest superheroes Alex, Julie, Jack, and Katie team up with their idols Wolverine, Cyclops, and the other X-Men to keep the world a safer place.
    "Marvel age"--Cover.
    Revision of the March 2006 issue of Marvel age X-Men Power Pack.
    ISBN-13: 978-1-59961-221-8
    ISBN-10: 1-59961-221-6
    1. Superheroes (Fictitious characters)--Comic books, strips, etc.--Fiction.
    2. Graphic novels. I. Title. II. Series.

741.5dc22

All Spotlight books are reinforced library binding and manufactured in the United States of America

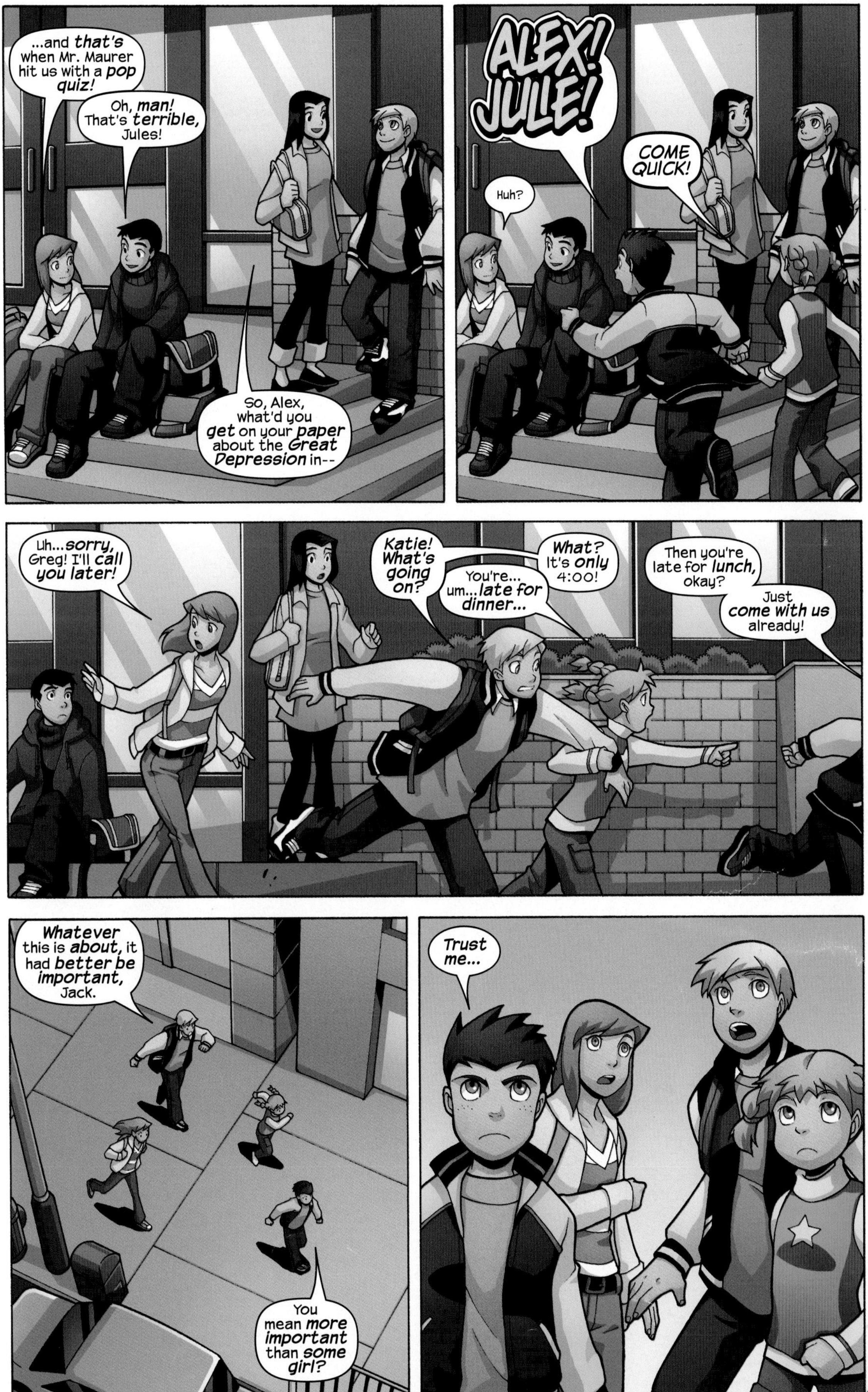
...and that's when Mr. Maurer hit us with a pop quiz!
Oh, man! That's terrible, Jules!
So, Alex, what'd you get on your paper about the Great Depression in--
ALEX! JULIE!
Huh?
COME QUICK!
Uh...sorry, Greg! I'll call you later!
Katie! What's going on?
You're... um...late for dinner...
What? It's only 4:00!
Then you're late for lunch, okay?
Just come with us already!
Whatever this is about, it had better be important, Jack.
You mean more important than some girl?
Trust me...

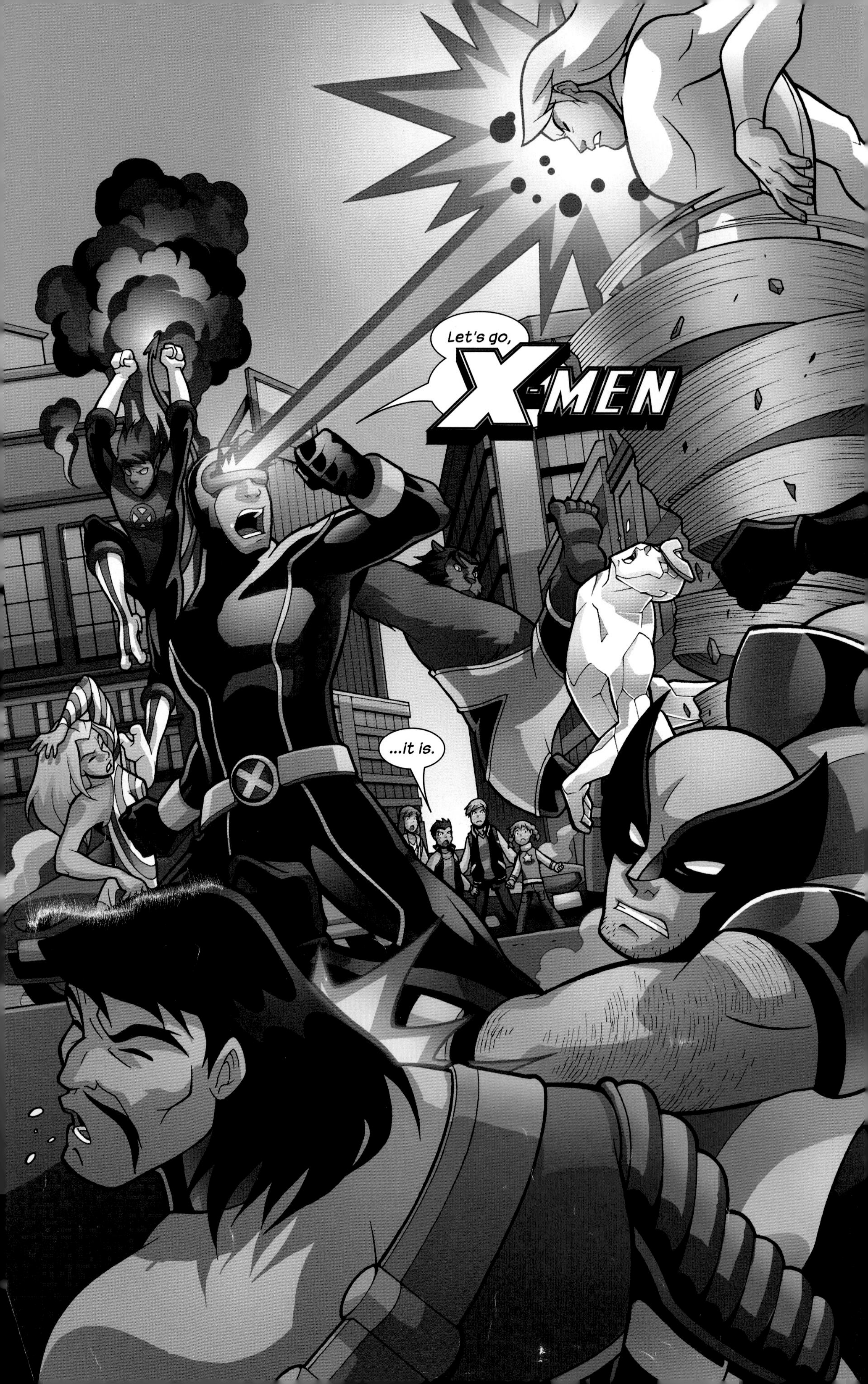
Let's go, X-MEN
...it is.

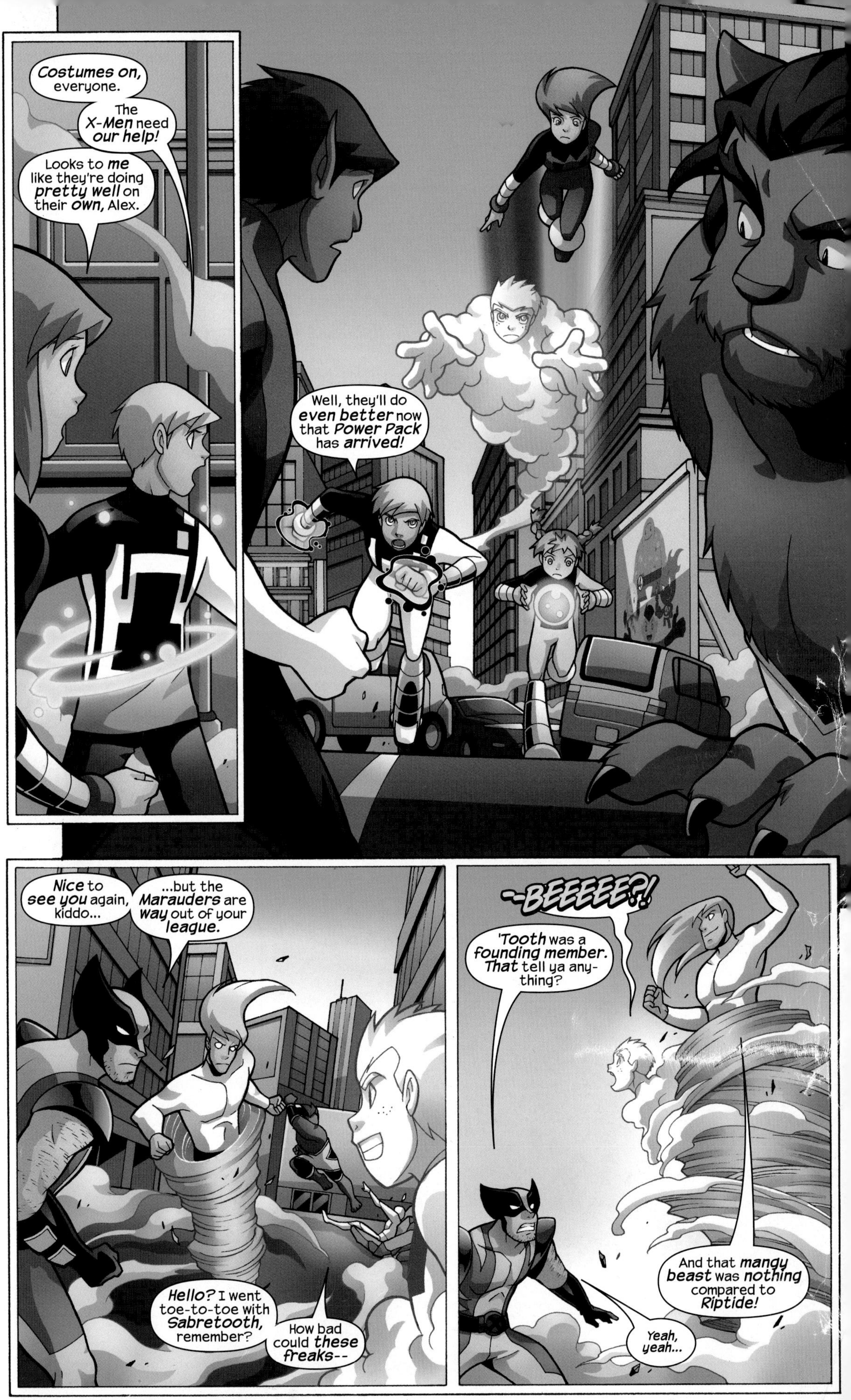
Costumes on, everyone.
The X-Men need our help!
Looks to me like they're doing pretty well on their own, Alex.
Well, they'll do even better now that Power Pack has arrived!
Nice to see you again, kiddo...
...but the Marauders are way out of your league.
Hello? I went toe-to-toe with Sabretooth, remember?
How bad could these freaks--
--BEEEEEE?!
'Tooth was a founding member. That tell ya any-thing?
And that mangy beast was nothing compared to Riptide!
Yeah, yeah...

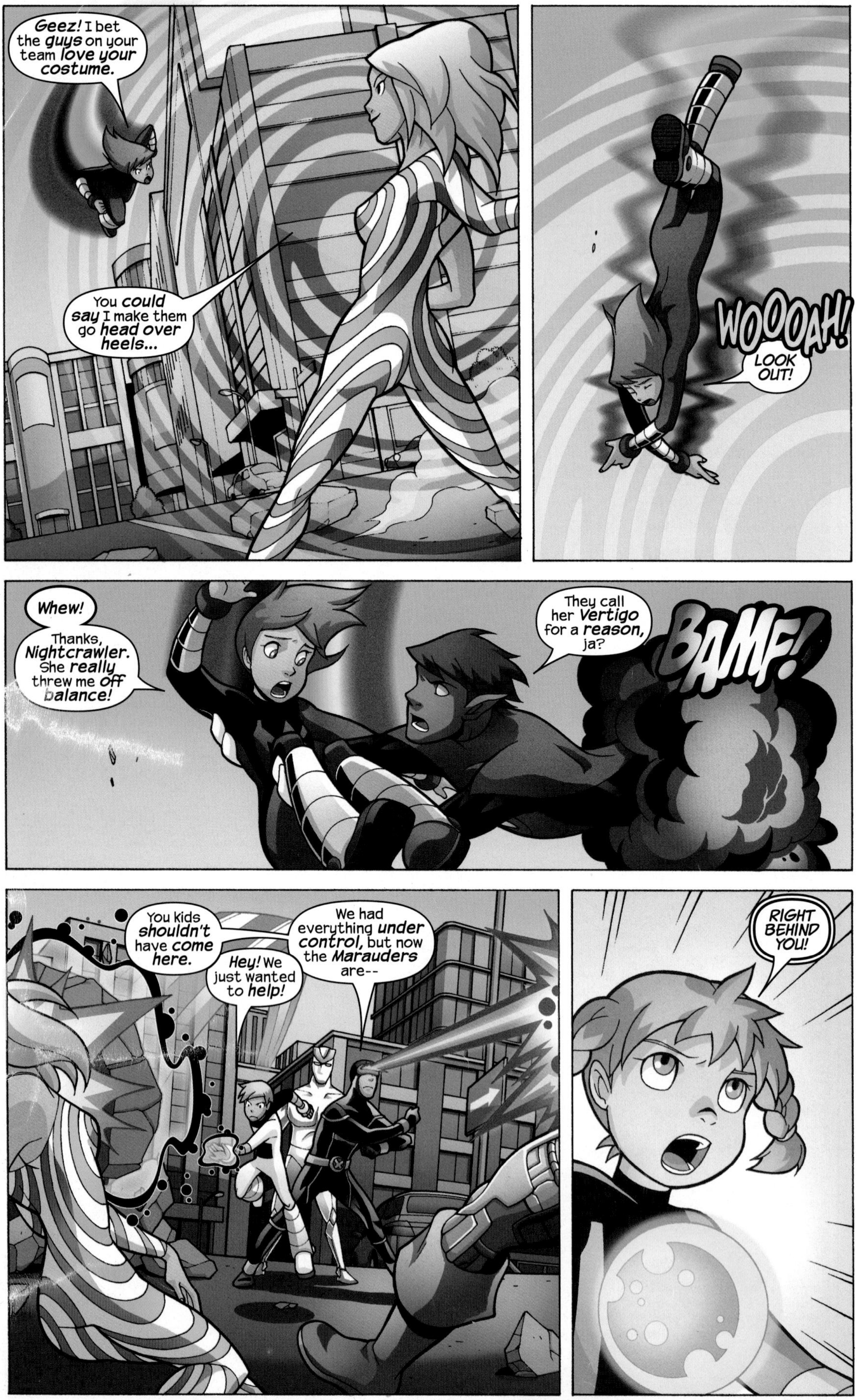
Geez! I bet the guys on your team love your costume.
You could say I make them go head over heels...
WOOOAH!
LOOK OUT!
Whew!
Thanks, Nightcrawler. She really threw me off balance!
They call her Vertigo for a reason, ja?
BAMF!
You kids shouldn't have come here.
Hey! We just wanted to help!
We had everything under control, but now the Marauders are--
RIGHT BEHIND YOU!

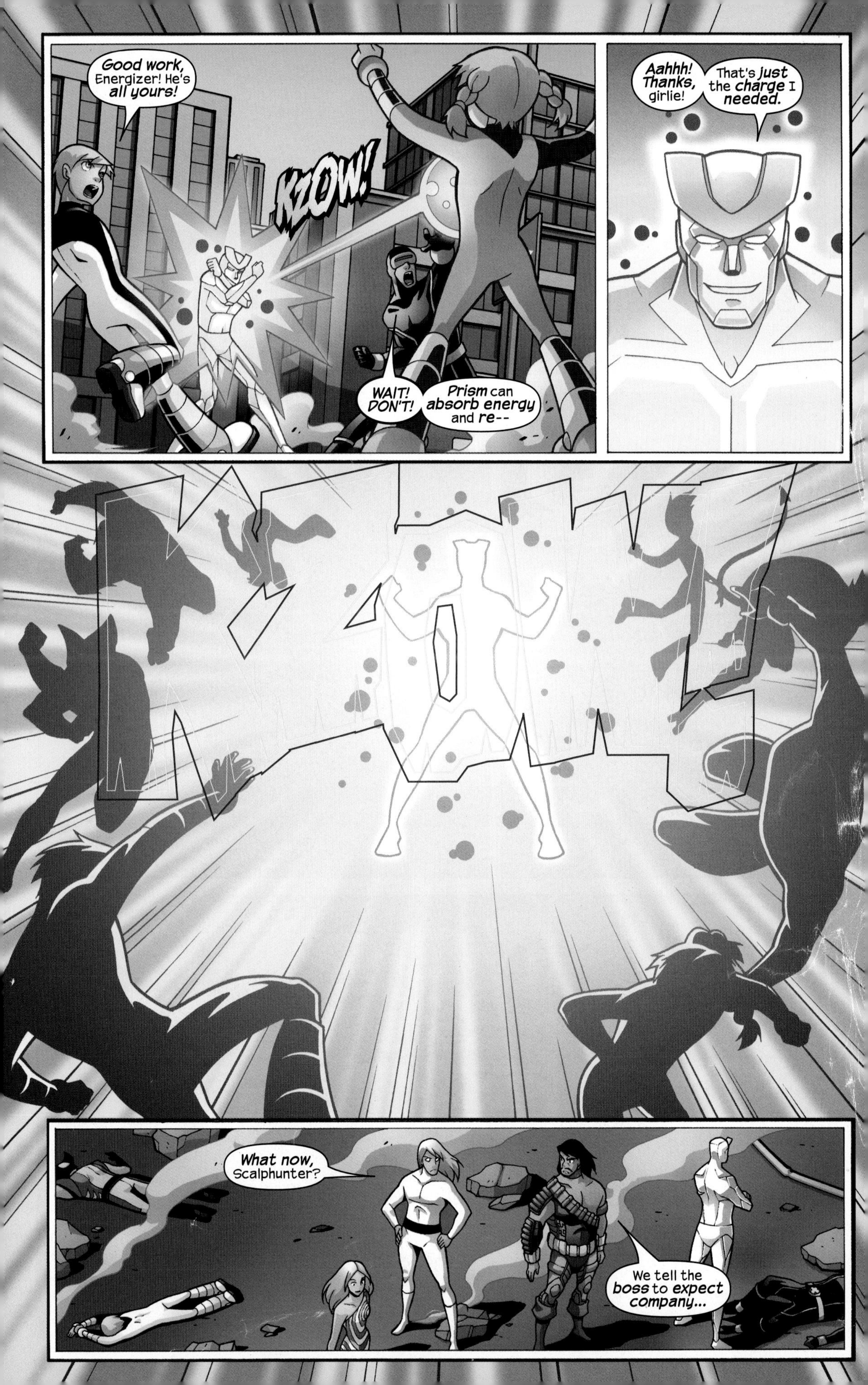
Good work, Energizer! He's all yours!
KZOW!
WAIT! DON'T!
Prism can absorb energy and re--
Aahhh! Thanks, girlie!
That's just the charge I needed.
What now, Scalphunter?
We tell the boss to expect company...

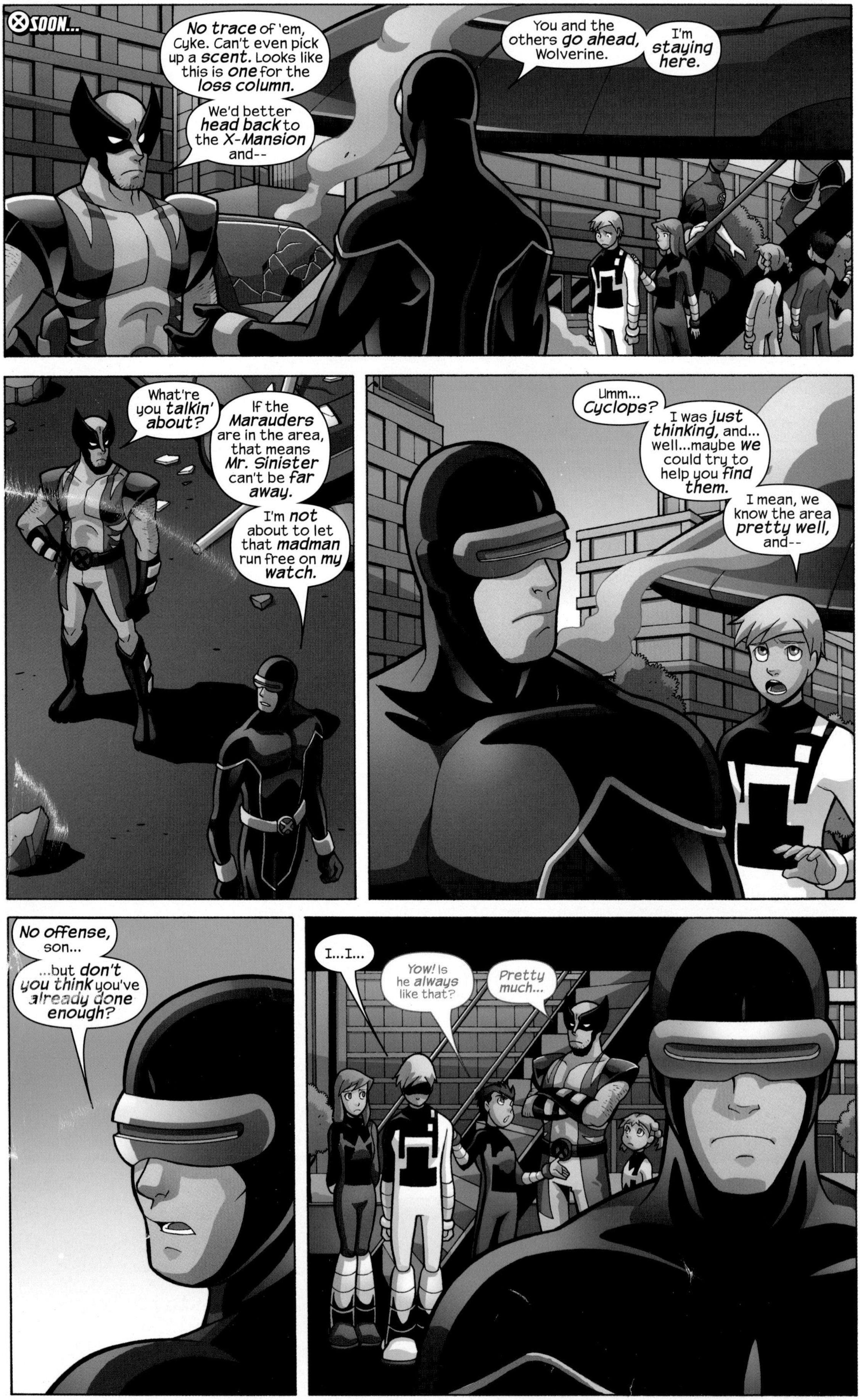
SOON...
No trace of 'em, Cyke. Can't even pick up a scent. Looks like this is one for the loss column.
We'd better head back to the X-Mansion and--
You and the others go ahead, Wolverine.
I'm staying here.
What're you talkin' about?
If the Marauders are in the area, that means Mr. Sinister can't be far away.
I'm not about to let that madman run free on my watch.
Umm... Cyclops?
I was just thinking, and... well...maybe we could try to help you find them.
I mean, we know the area pretty well, and--
No offense, son...
...but don't you think you've already done enough?
I...I...
Yow! Is he always like that?
Pretty much...

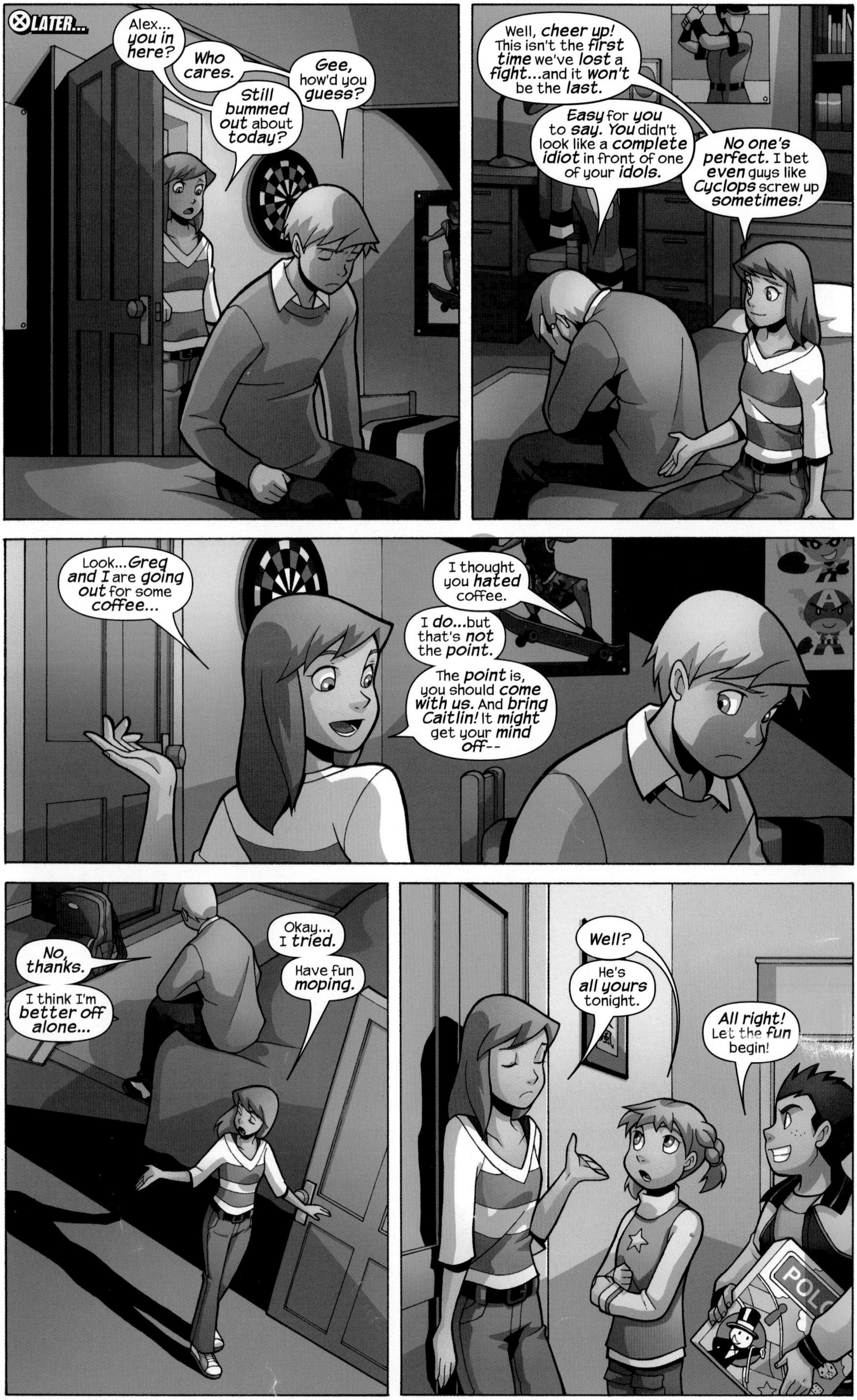
LATER...
Alex... you in here?
Who cares.
Still bummed out about today?
Gee, how'd you guess?
Well, cheer up! This isn't the first time we've lost a fight...and it won't be the last.
Easy for you to say. You didn't look like a complete idiot in front of one of your idols.
No one's perfect. I bet even guys like Cyclops screw up sometimes!
Look...Greg and I are going out for some coffee...
I thought you hated coffee.
I do...but that's not the point.
The point is, you should come with us. And bring Caitlin! It might get your mind off--
No, thanks.
I think I'm better off alone...
Okay... I tried.
Have fun moping.
Well?
He's all yours tonight.
All right! Let the fun begin!

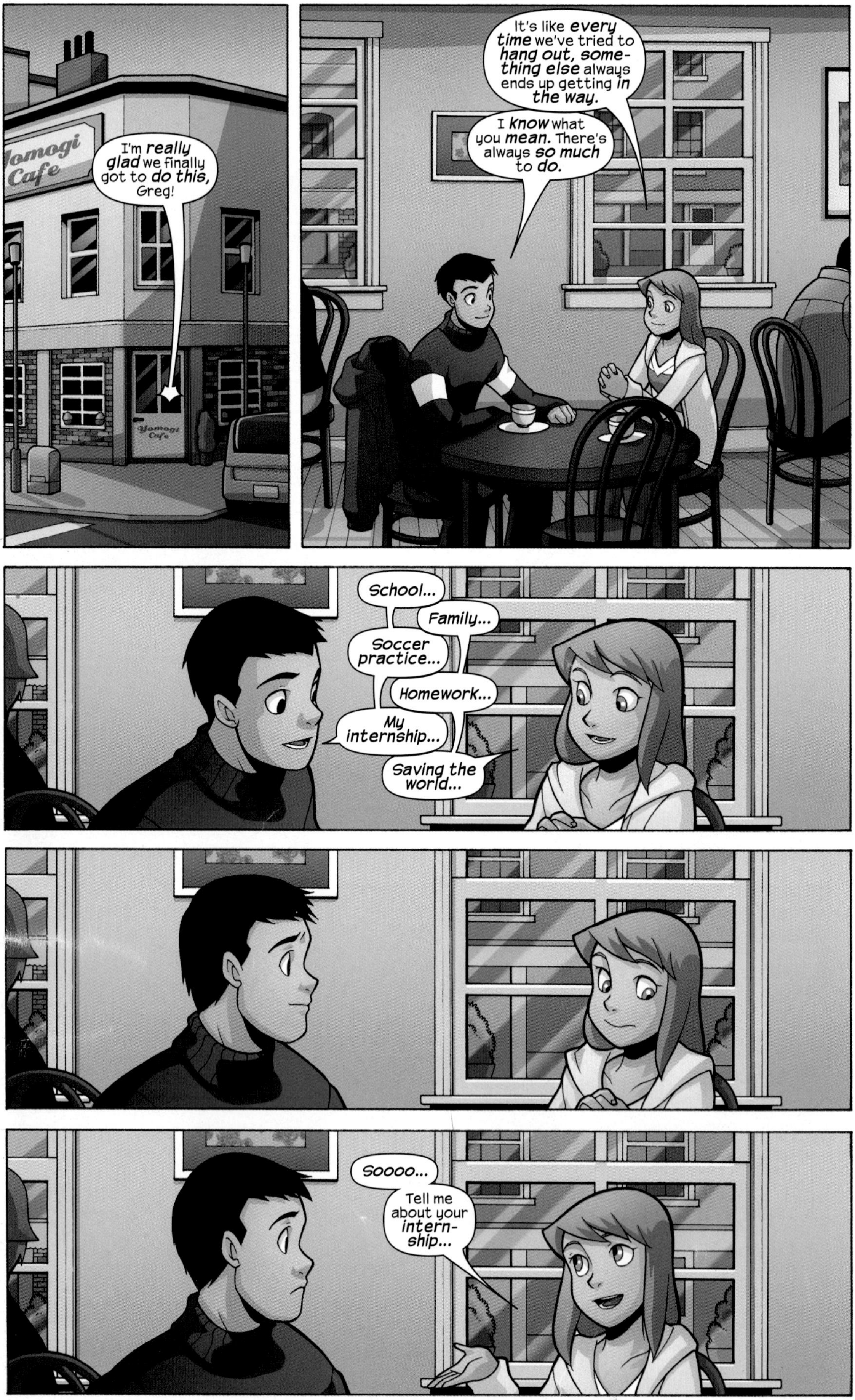
I'm really glad we finally got to do this, Greg!
Yomogi Cafe
It's like every time we've tried to hang out, something else always ends up getting in the way.
I know what you mean. There's always so much to do.
School...
Family...
Soccer practice...
Homework...
My internship...
Saving the world...
Soooo...
Tell me about your internship...

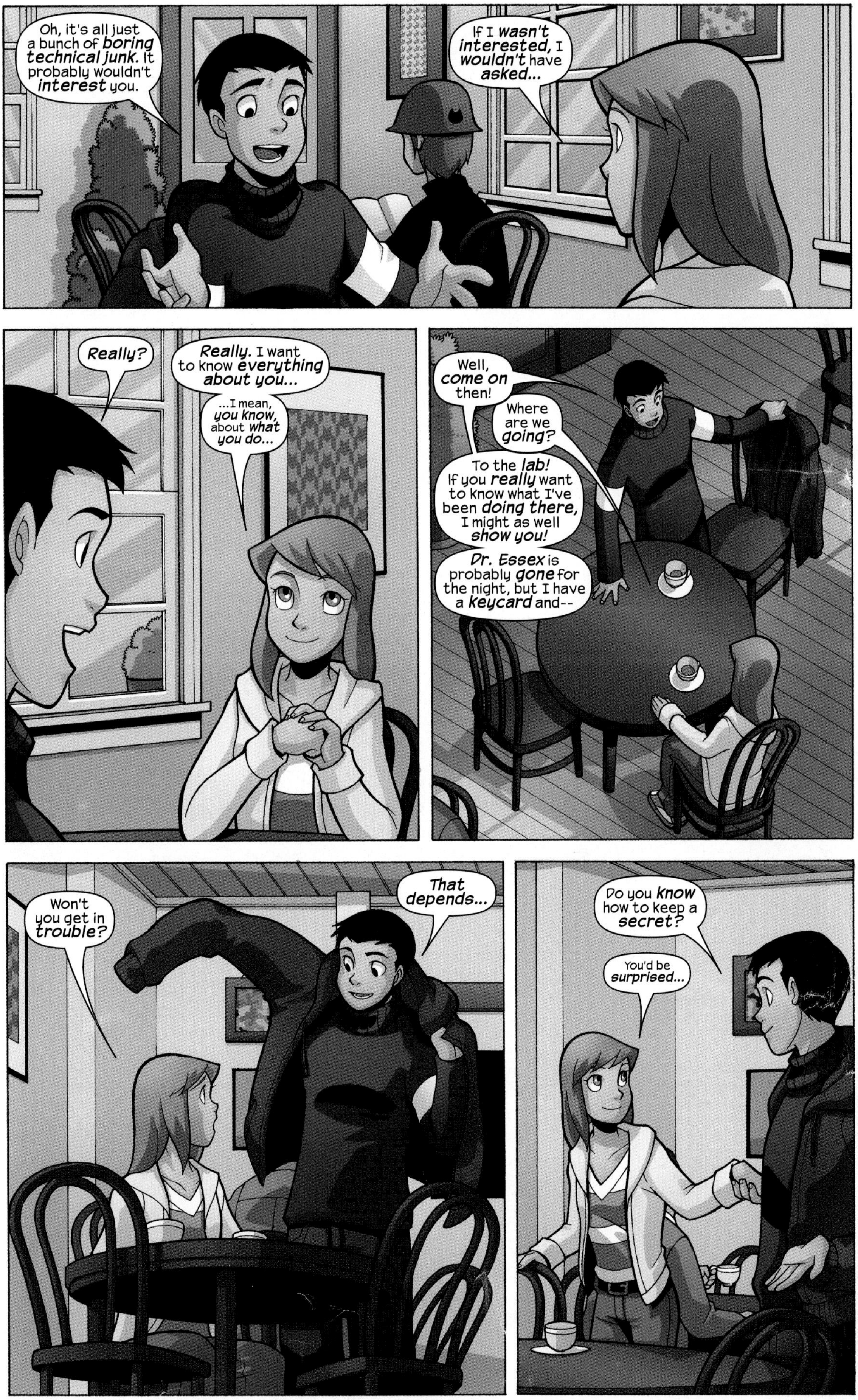
Oh, it's all just a bunch of boring technical junk. It probably wouldn't interest you.
If I wasn't interested, I wouldn't have asked...
Really?
Really. I want to know everything about you...
...I mean, you know, about what you do...
Well, come on then!
Where are we going?
To the lab! If you really want to know what I've been doing there, I might as well show you!
Dr. Essex is probably gone for the night, but I have a keycard and--
Won't you get in trouble?
That depends...
Do you know how to keep a secret?
You'd be surprised...

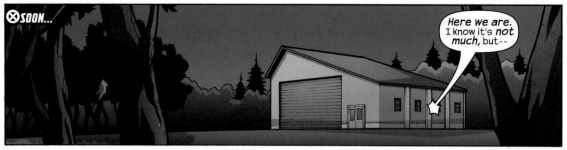

Here we are. I know it's *not much,* but--

Are you *kidding?* Look at all of this stuff!

It's *so cool!*

Yeah, I guess it's *not too shabby.*

I've been *pretty much running this place by myself* lately and--

Hey! Is this a *spectral radiometer?* My *dad* has--

Whoa! Put that down!

If we *touch* anything I'm gonna be in *big* trouble!

I thought you were "pretty much running this place by yourself"...

I...um... I may have *exaggerated* a *little bit.*

You must think I'm a *total dork.*

Actually, I think it's *kinda cute.*

Julie, there's *something* I've been meaning to *tell you...*

I...well...I *really* like you. *A lot.* And I was--I was *kinda hoping* you'd maybe like to be my--

SLAM

--*DUCK!*

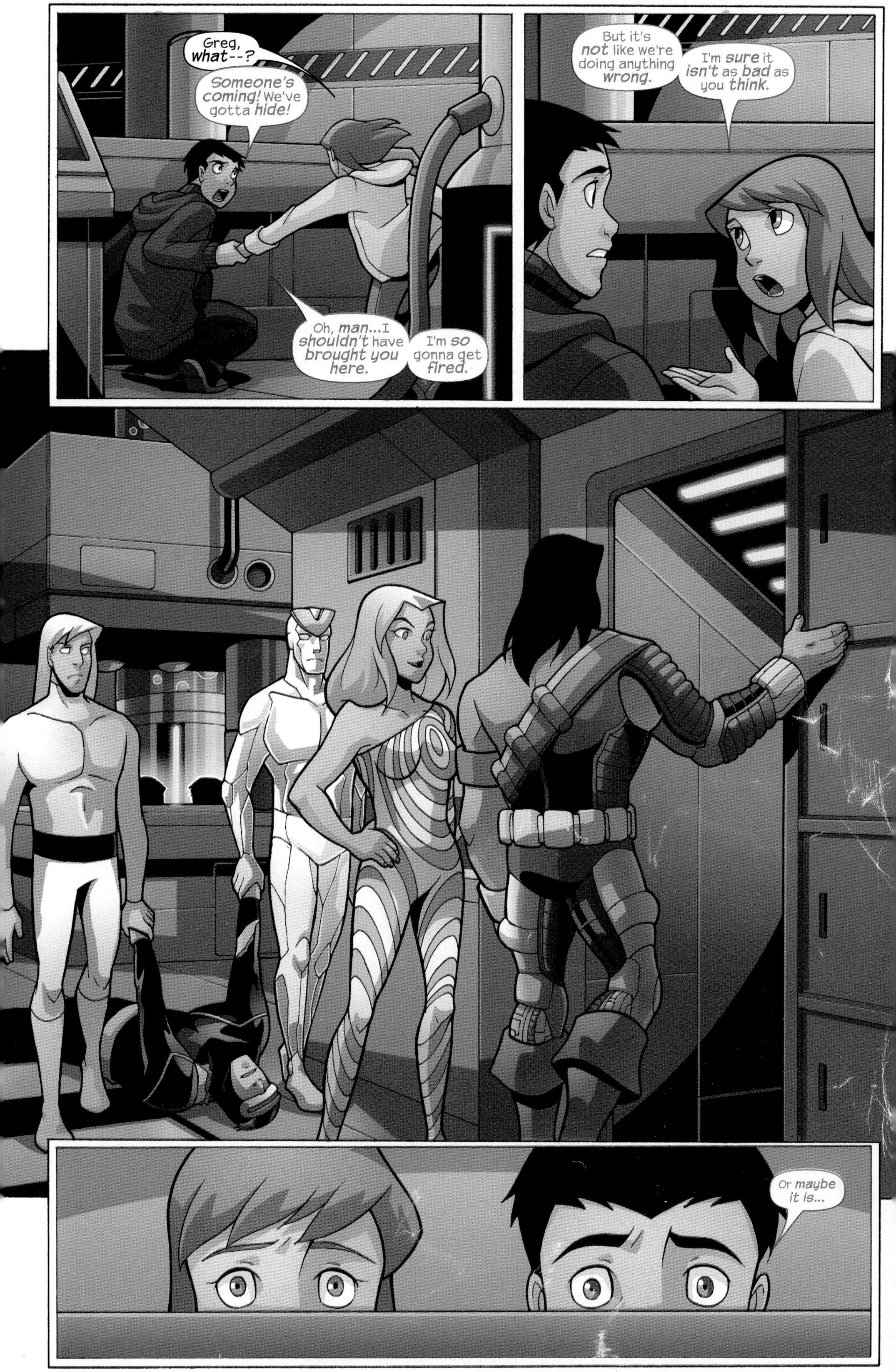
Greg, what--?
Someone's coming! We've gotta hide!
Oh, man...I shouldn't have brought you here.
I'm so gonna get fired.
But it's not like we're doing anything wrong.
I'm sure it isn't as bad as you think.
Or maybe it is...

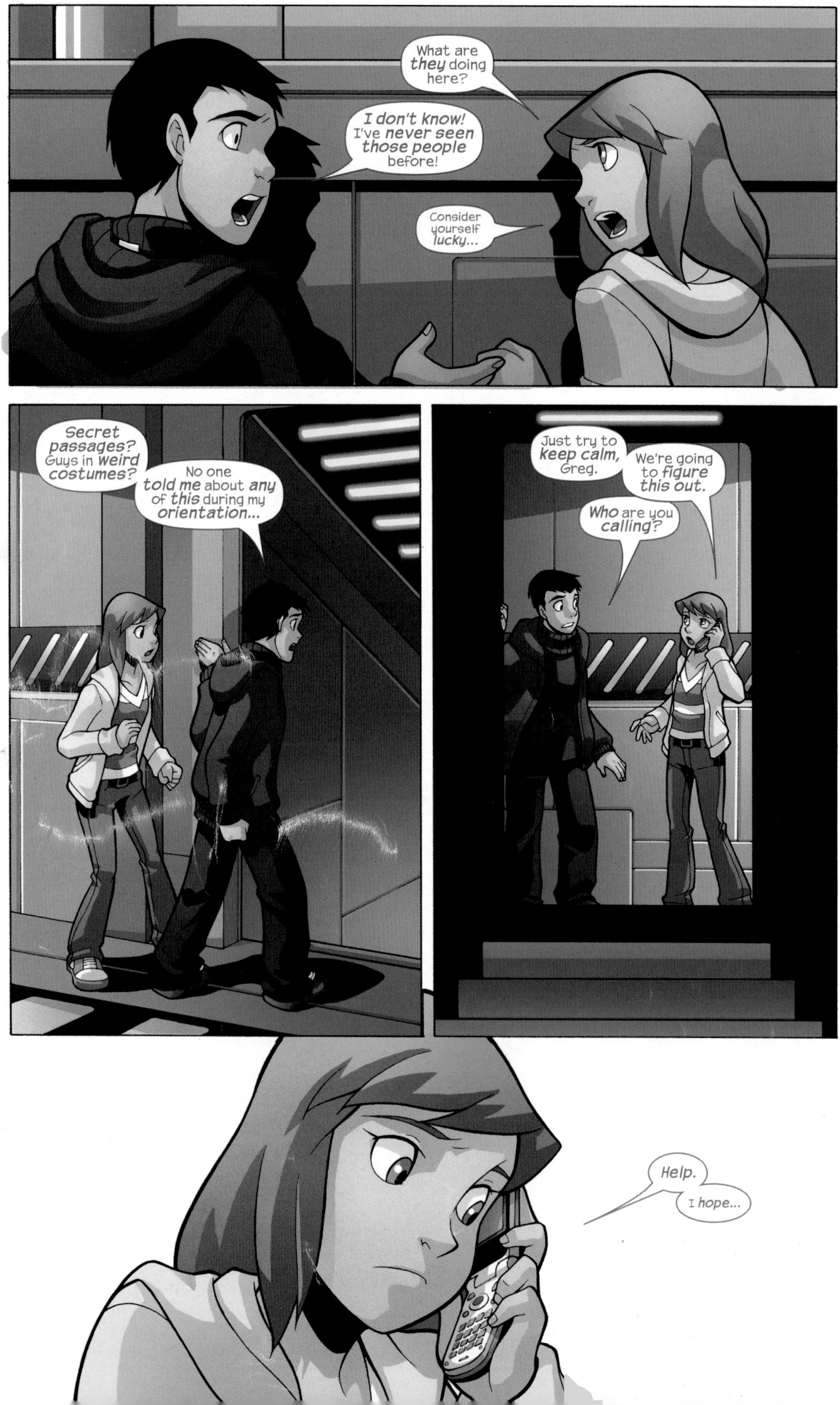
What are they doing here?
I don't know! I've never seen those people before!
Consider yourself lucky...
Secret passages? Guys in weird costumes?
No one told me about any of this during my orientation...
Just try to keep calm, Greg.
We're going to figure this out.
Who are you calling?
Help.
I hope...

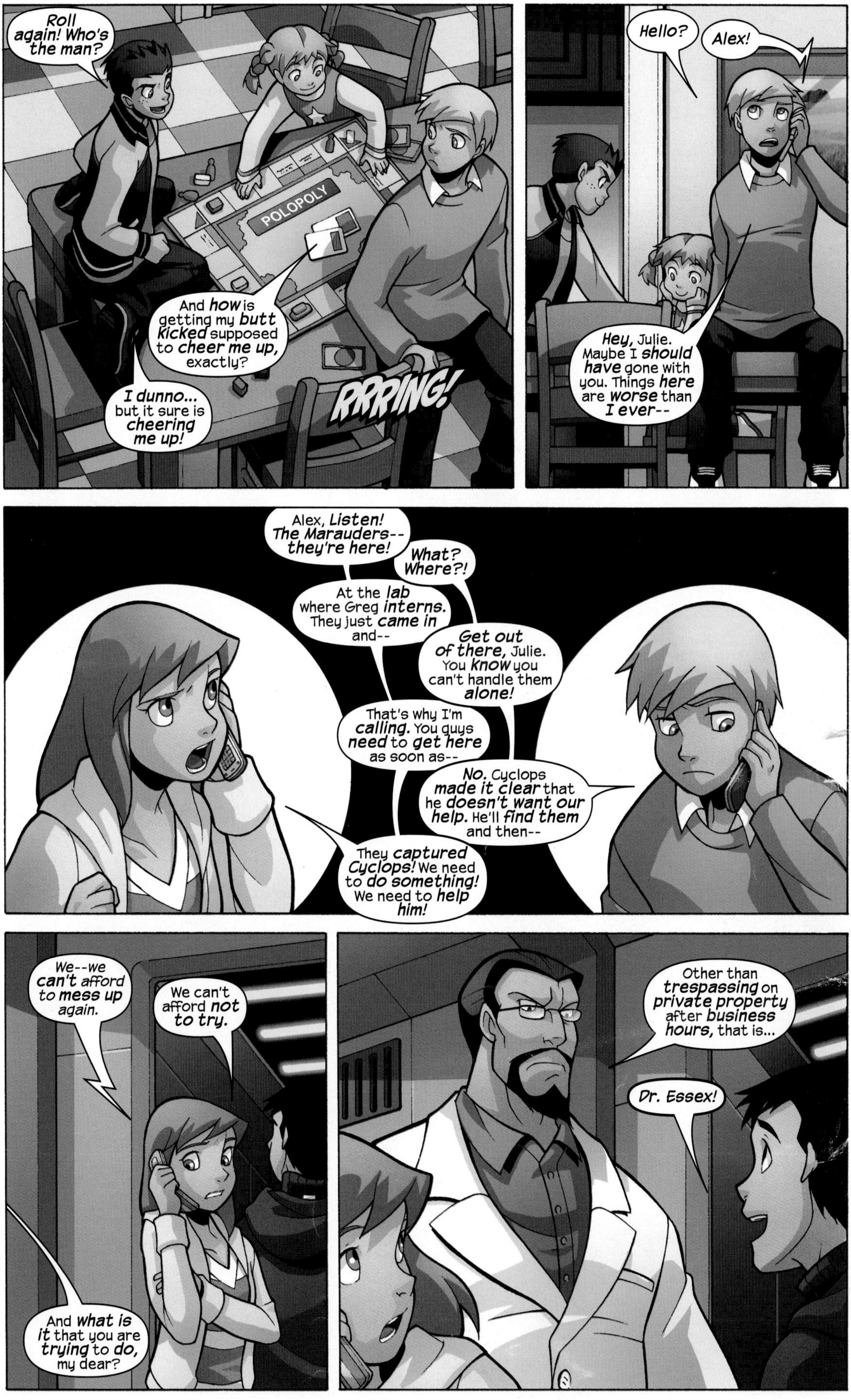
Roll again! Who's the man?
POLOPOLY
And how is getting my butt kicked supposed to cheer me up, exactly?
I dunno... but it sure is cheering me up!
RRRING!
Hello?
Alex!
Hey, Julie. Maybe I should have gone with you. Things here are worse than I ever--
Alex, Listen! The Marauders-- they're here!
What? Where?!
At the lab where Greg interns. They just came in and--
Get out of there, Julie. You know you can't handle them alone!
That's why I'm calling. You guys need to get here as soon as--
No. Cyclops made it clear that he doesn't want our help. He'll find them and then--
They captured Cyclops! We need to do something! We need to help him!
We--we can't afford to mess up again.
We can't afford not to try.
And what is it that you are trying to do, my dear?
Other than trespassing on private property after business hours, that is...
Dr. Essex!

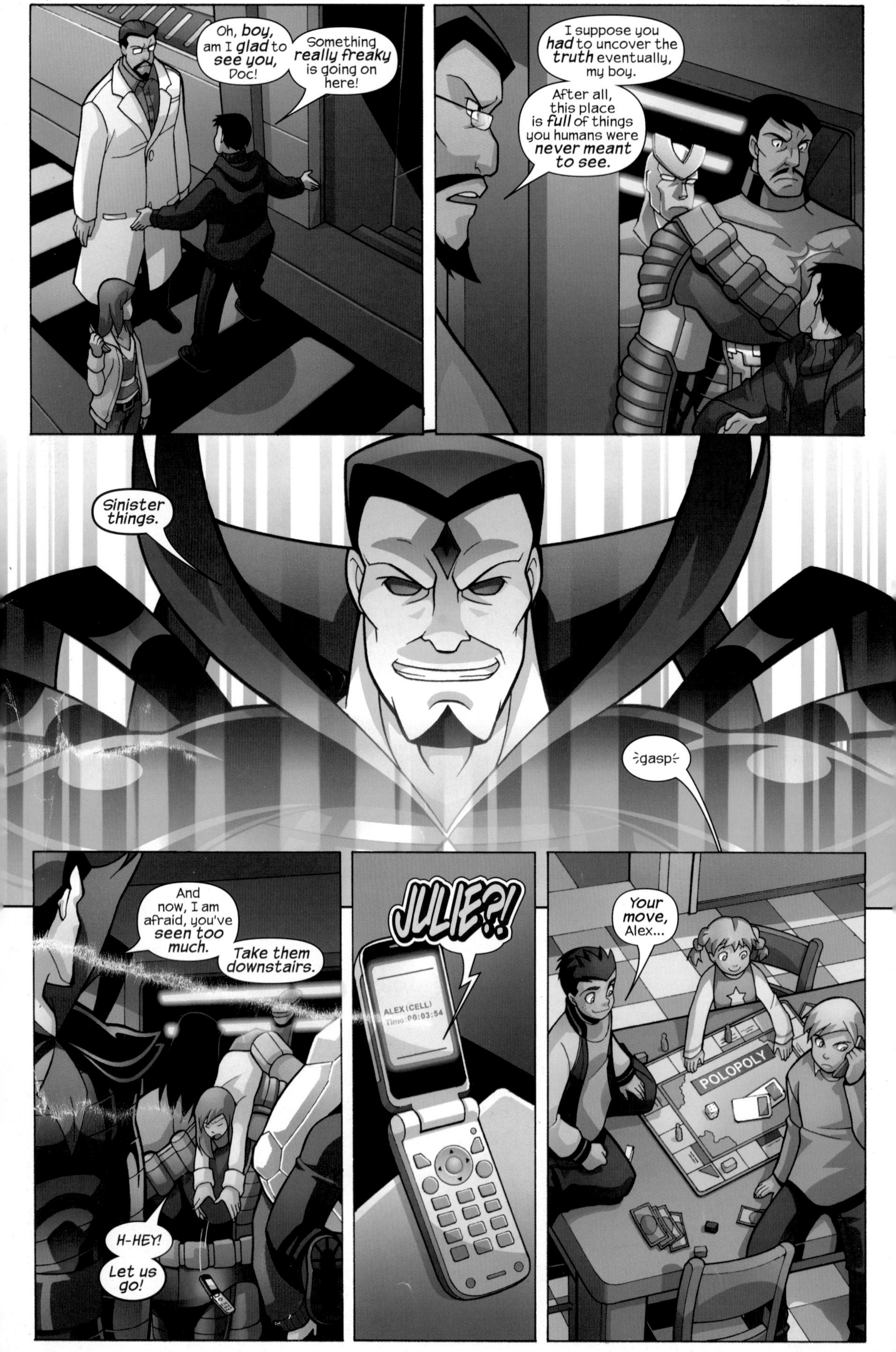
Oh, boy, am I glad to see you, Doc!
Something really freaky is going on here!
I suppose you had to uncover the truth eventually, my boy.
After all, this place is full of things you humans were never meant to see.
Sinister things.
-gasp-
And now, I am afraid, you've seen too much.
Take them downstairs.
H-HEY!
Let us go!
JULIE?!
ALEX (CELL)
Time 00:03:54
Your move, Alex...
POLOPOLY

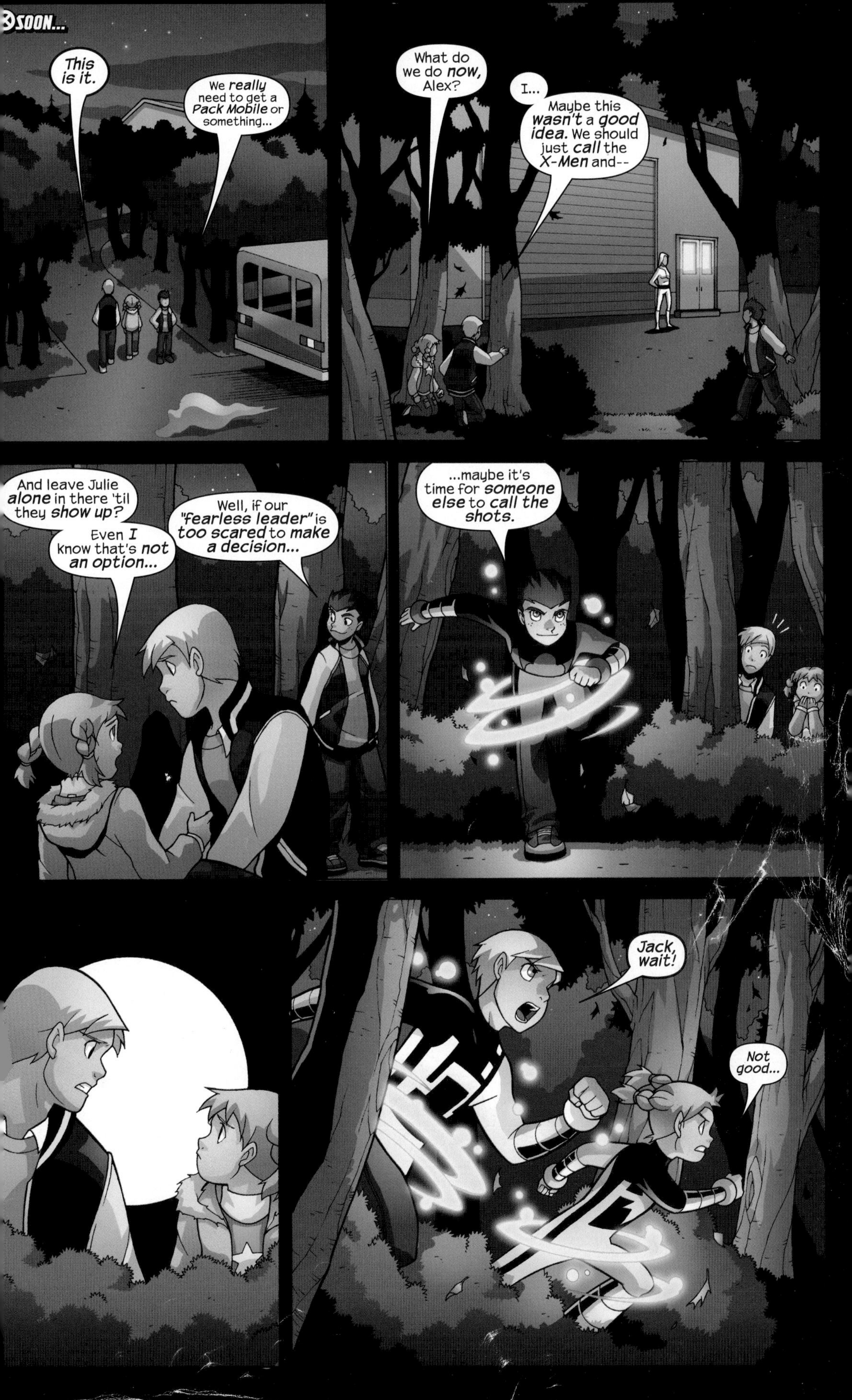
SOON...
This is it.
We really need to get a Pack Mobile or something...
What do we do now, Alex?
I...
Maybe this wasn't a good idea. We should just call the X-Men and--
And leave Julie alone in there 'til they show up?
Even I know that's not an option...
Well, if our "fearless leader" is too scared to make a decision...
...maybe it's time for someone else to call the shots.
Jack, wait!
Not good...

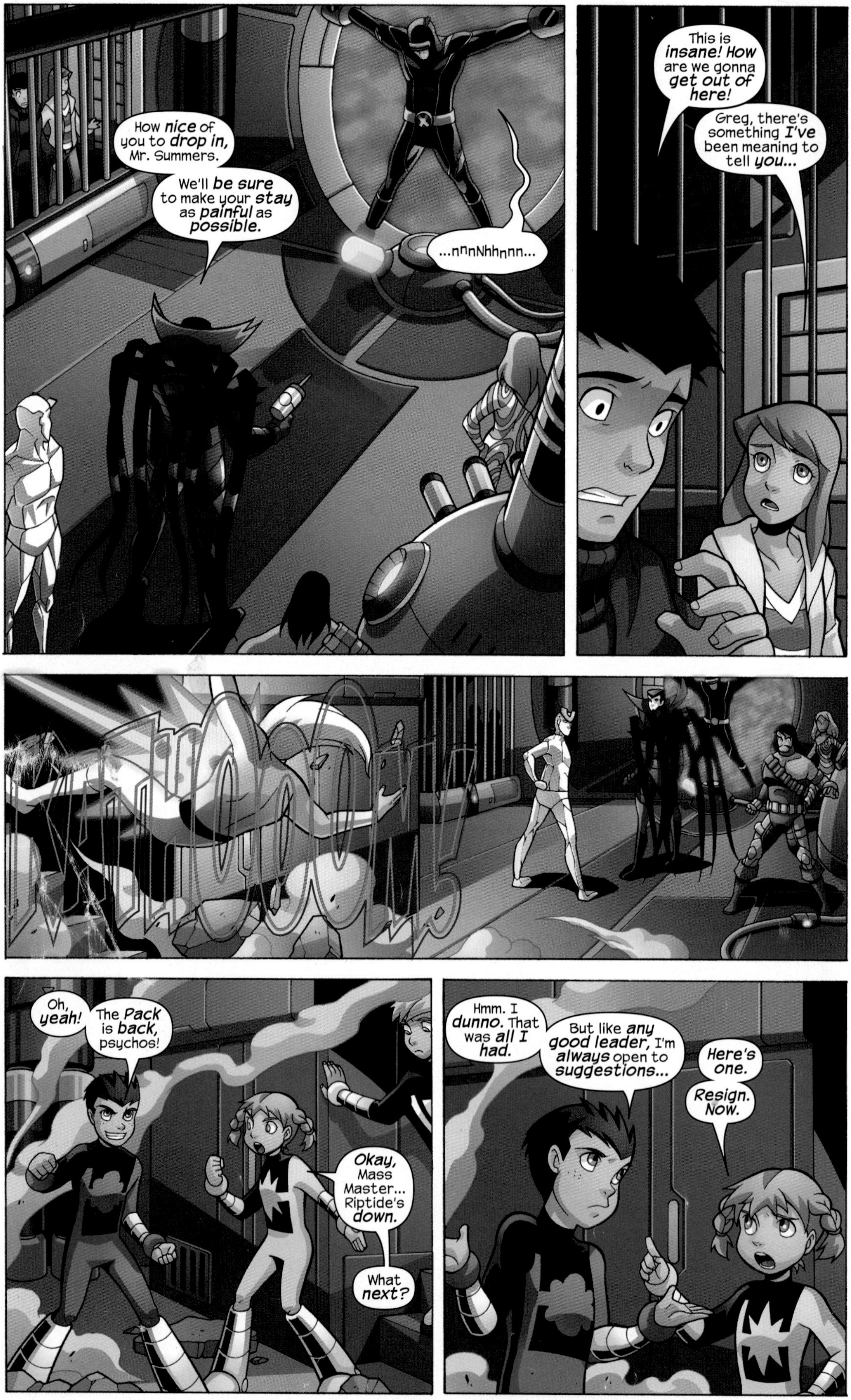
How nice of you to drop in, Mr. Summers.
We'll be sure to make your stay as painful as possible.
...nnnNhhnnn...
This is insane! How are we gonna get out of here!
Greg, there's something I've been meaning to tell you...
Oh, yeah!
The Pack is back, psychos!
Okay, Mass Master... Riptide's down.
What next?
Hmm. I dunno. That was all I had.
But like any good leader, I'm always open to suggestions...
Here's one.
Resign. Now.

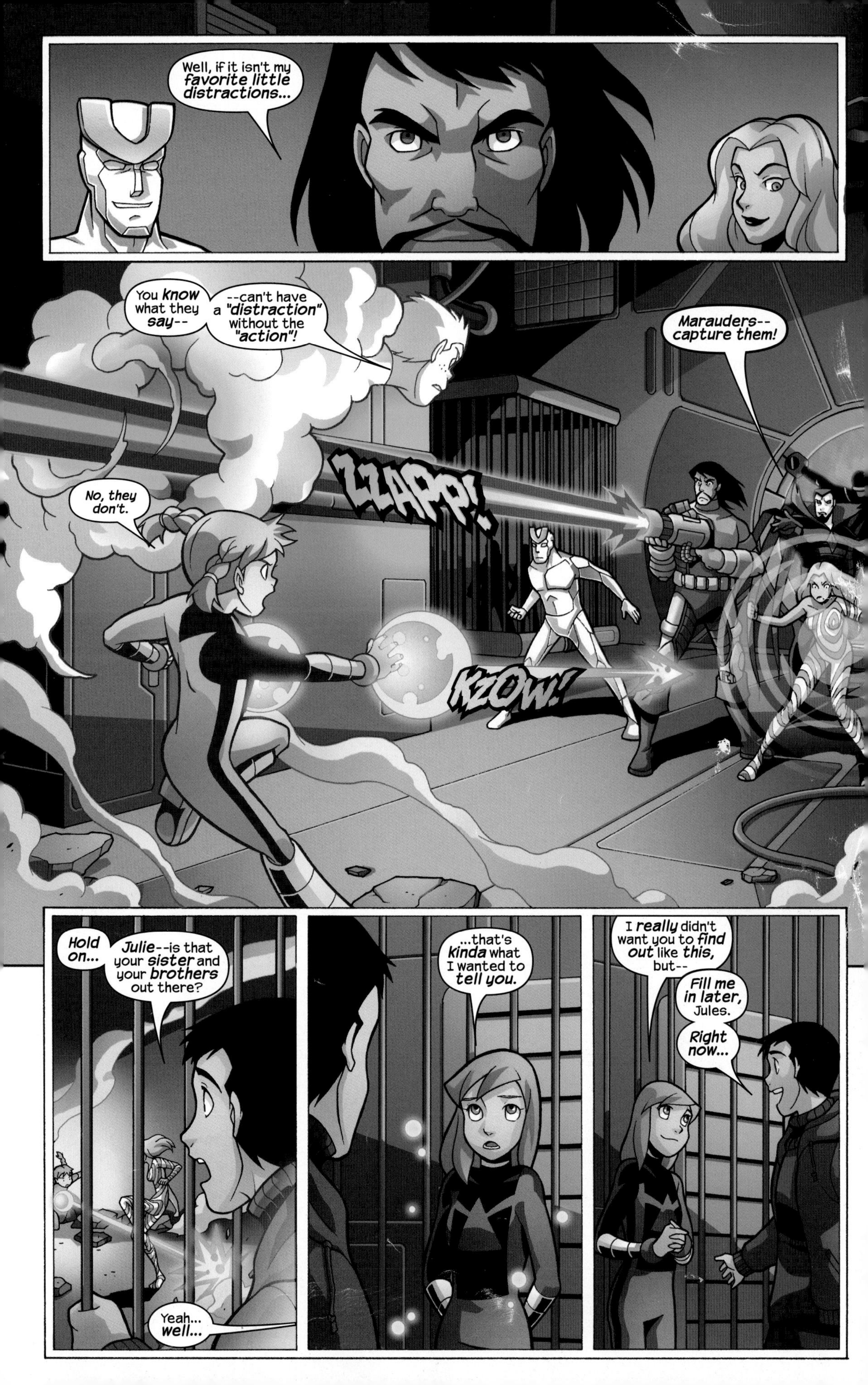

Well, if it isn't my favorite little distractions...
You know what they say--
--can't have a "distraction" without the "action"!
Marauders--capture them!
No, they don't.
ZZAPP!
KZOW!
Hold on...
Julie--is that your sister and your brothers out there?
Yeah... well...
...that's kinda what I wanted to tell you.
I really didn't want you to find out like this, but--
Fill me in later, Jules.
Right now...

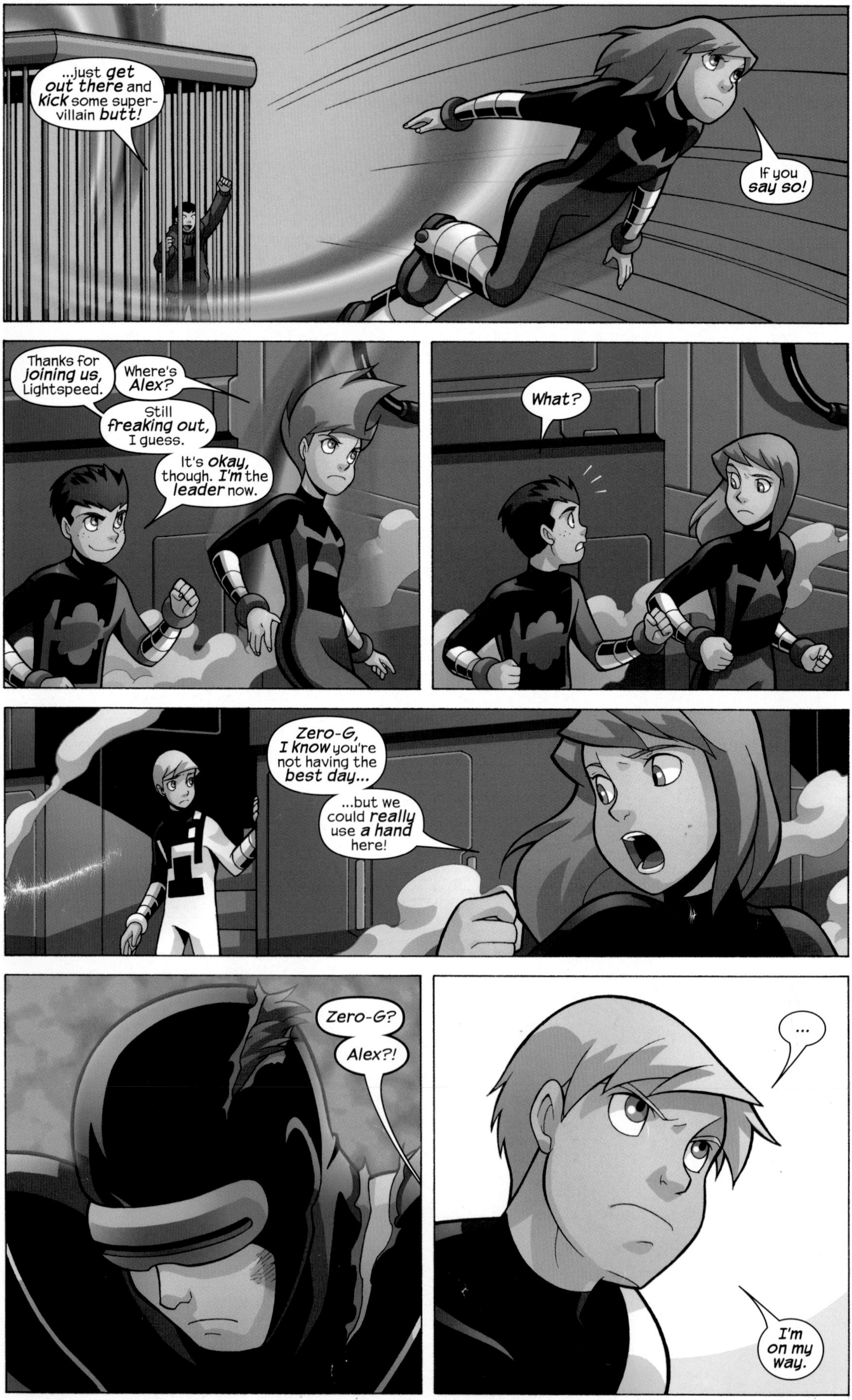
...just get out there and kick some super-villain butt!
If you say so!
Thanks for joining us, Lightspeed.
Where's Alex?
Still freaking out, I guess.
It's okay, though. I'm the leader now.
What?
Zero-G, I know you're not having the best day...
...but we could really use a hand here!
Zero-G?
Alex?!
...
I'm on my way.

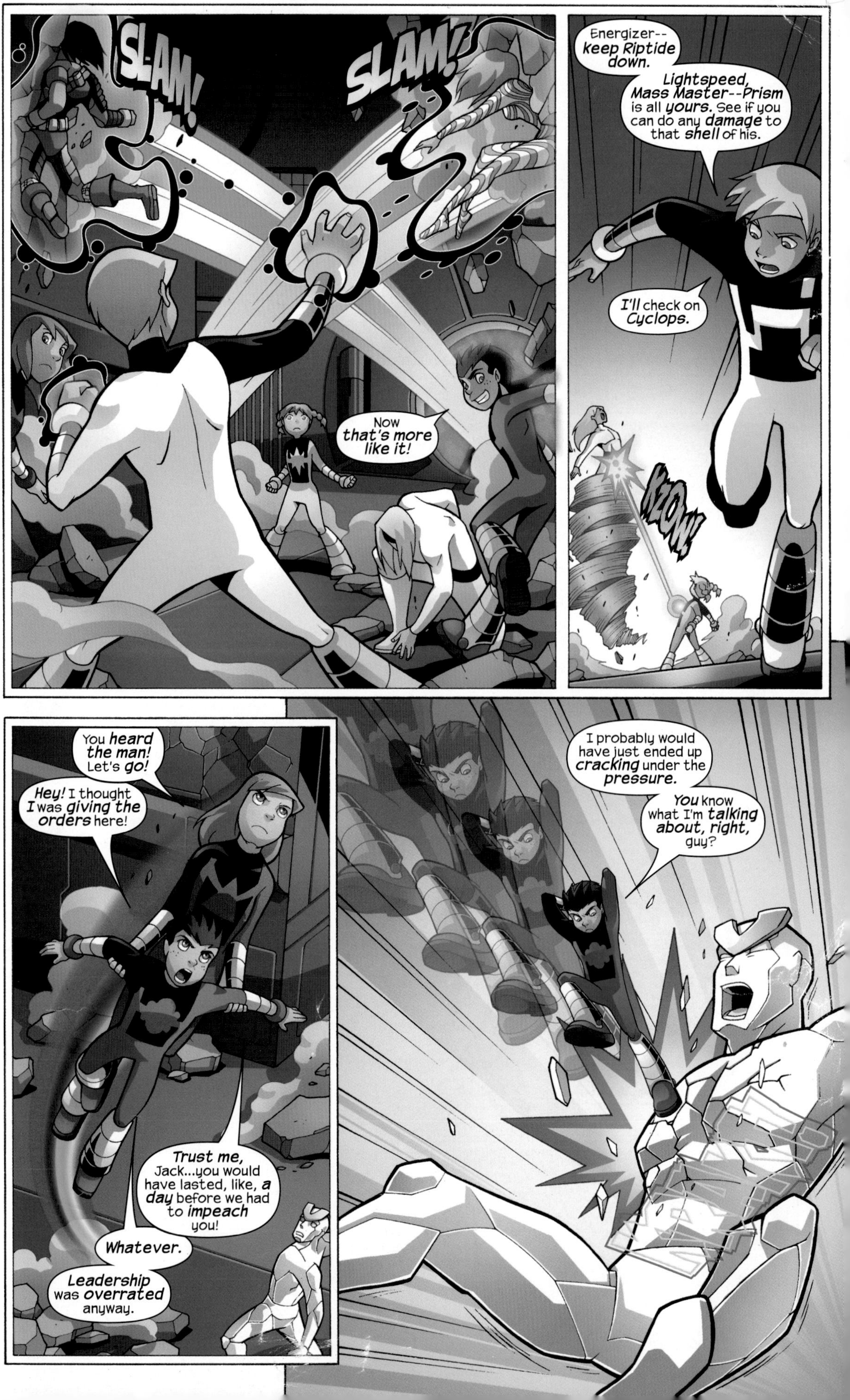
SLAM!
SLAM!
Now that's more like it!
Energizer-- keep Riptide down.
Lightspeed, Mass Master--Prism is all yours. See if you can do any damage to that shell of his.
I'll check on Cyclops.
KZOW!
You heard the man! Let's go!
Hey! I thought I was giving the orders here!
Trust me, Jack...you would have lasted, like, a day before we had to impeach you!
Whatever.
Leadership was overrated anyway.
I probably would have just ended up cracking under the pressure.
You know what I'm talking about, right, guy?

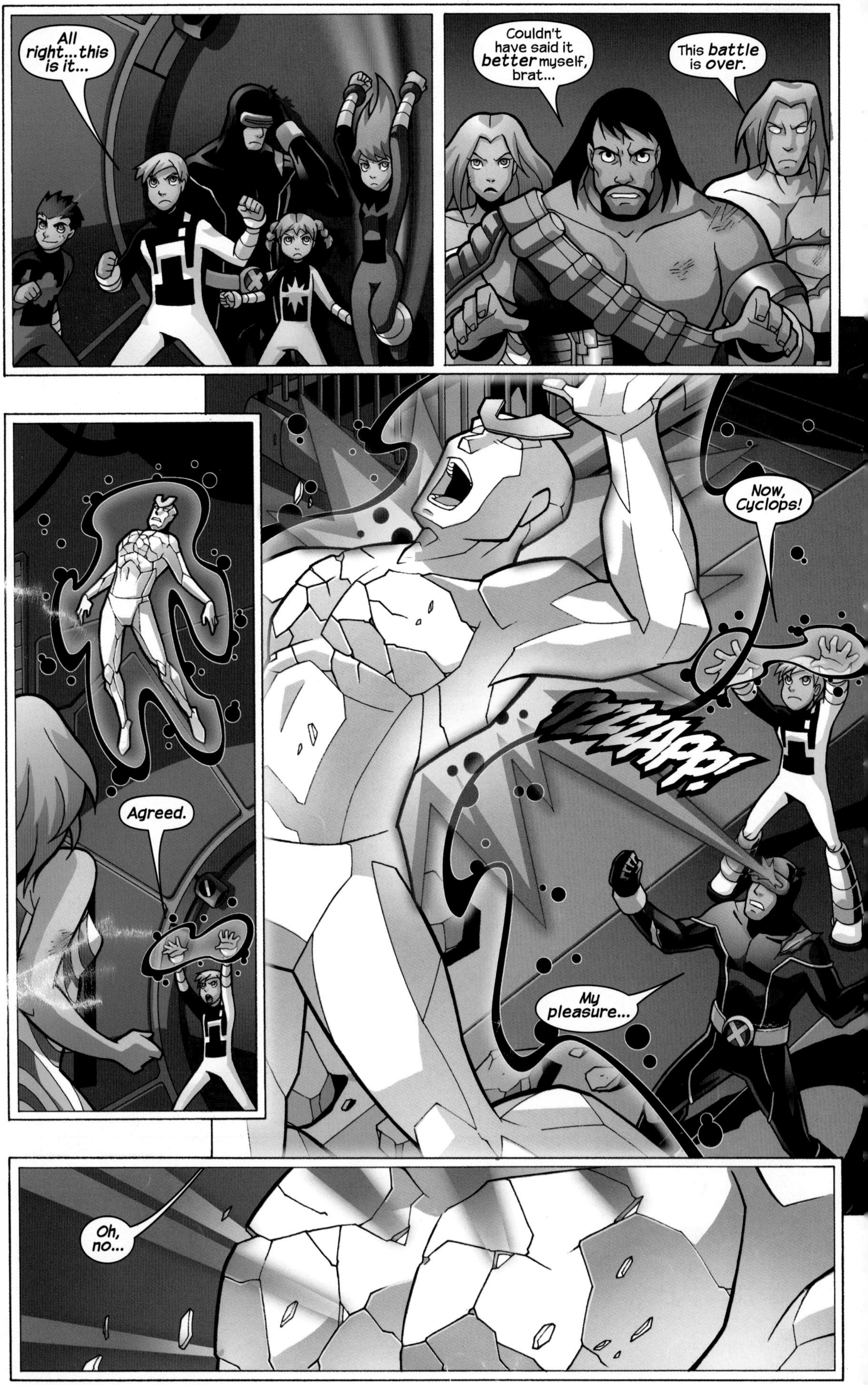
All right...this is it...
Couldn't have said it better myself, brat...
This battle is over.
Agreed.
Now, Cyclops!
My pleasure...
Oh, no...

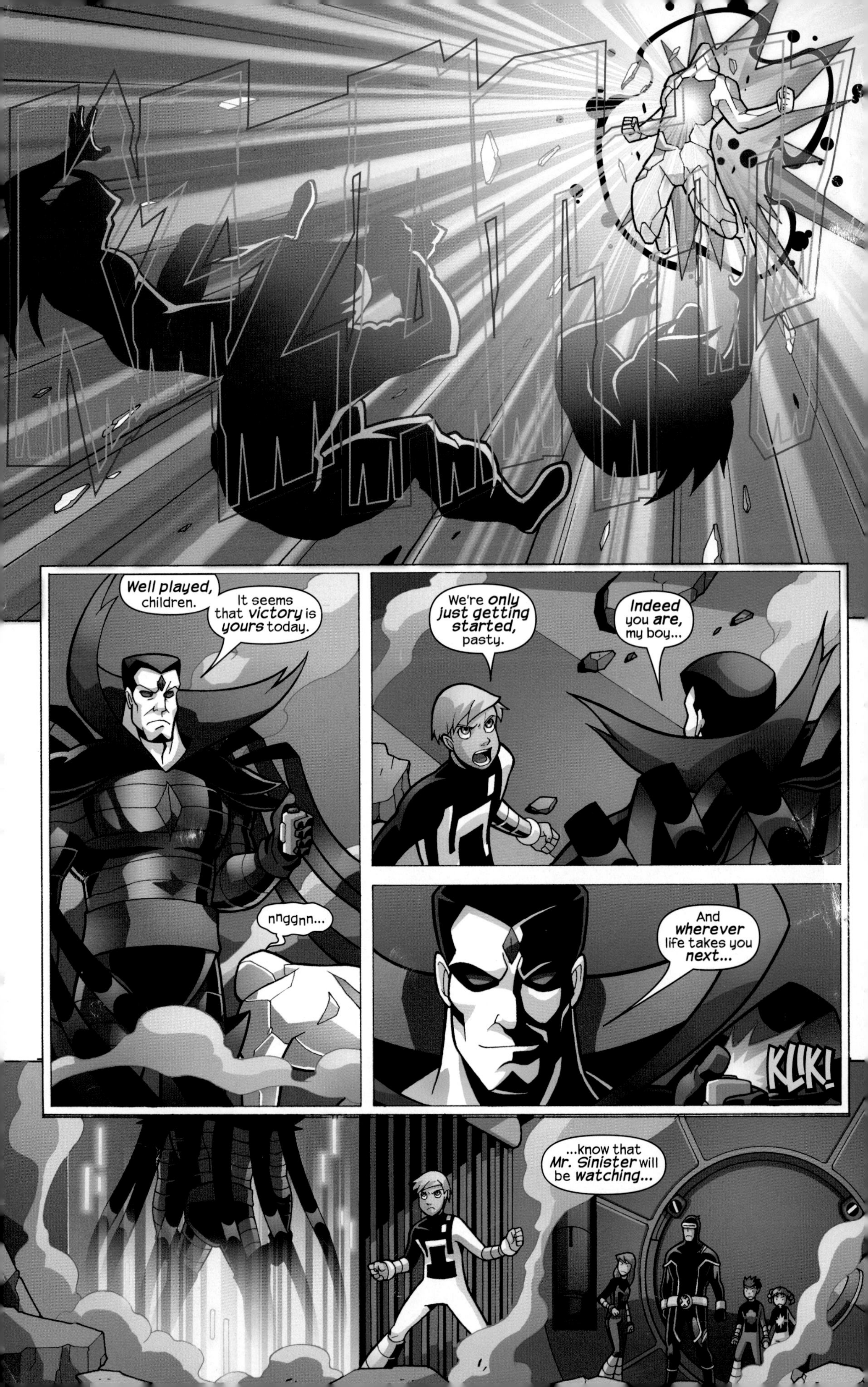
Well played, children.
It seems that victory is yours today.
nnggnn...
We're only just getting started, pasty.
Indeed you are, my boy...
And wherever life takes you next...
KLIK!
...know that Mr. Sinister will be watching...

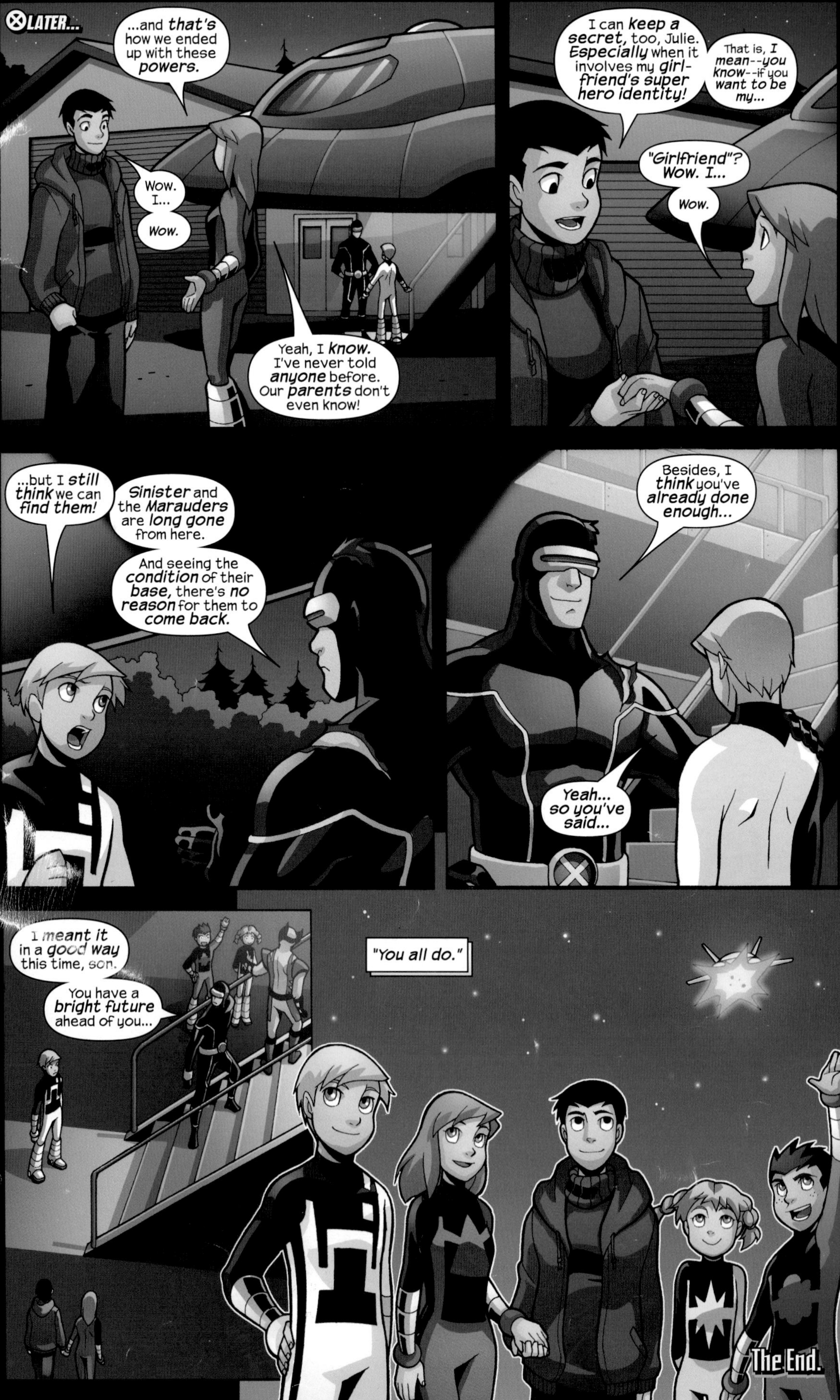
LATER...
...and that's how we ended up with these powers.
Wow. I...
Wow.
Yeah, I know. I've never told anyone before. Our parents don't even know!
I can keep a secret, too, Julie. Especially when it involves my girlfriend's super hero identity!
That is, I mean--you know--if you want to be my...
"Girlfriend"? Wow. I...
Wow.
...but I still think we can find them!
Sinister and the Marauders are long gone from here.
And seeing the condition of their base, there's no reason for them to come back.
Besides, I think you've already done enough...
Yeah... so you've said...
I meant it in a good way this time, son.
You have a bright future ahead of you...
"You all do."
The End.

JUL 2 4 2008.

21 70

DISCARD